THE STORY OF
Mrs. Lovewright
AND
Purrless Her Cat

by LORE SEGAL

illustrations by
PAUL O. ZELINSKY

ALFRED A. KNOPF   New York

For Sarah in Los Angeles
For Dallas in Evanston
L. S.

For Sbuj
P. O. Z.

This is a Borzoi Book
Published by Alfred A. Knopf, Inc.

Text copyright © 1985 by Lore Segal
Illustrations copyright © 1985 by Paul O. Zelinsky
All rights reserved under International and Pan-American
Copyright Conventions. Published in the United States
by Alfred A. Knopf, Inc., New York, and simultaneously
in Canada by Random House of Canada Limited, Toronto.
Distributed by Random House, Inc., New York.
Manufactured in the United States of America
2 4 6 8 0 9 7 5 3 1
First Edition

Library of Congress Cataloging in Publication Data
Segal, Lore Groszmann.
The story of Mrs. Lovewright and Purrless her cat.
Summary: Mrs. Lovewright is sure that a cat is just
what she needs until she acquires a cat that
has a mind of its own.
1. Children's stories, American.   [1. Cats—Fiction]
I. Zelinsky, Paul O., ill.   II. Title.
PZ7.S4527Ss 1985 [E] 84-25011
ISBN 0-394-86817-X
ISBN 0-394-96817-4 (lib. bdg.)

Mrs. Lovewright was a chilly person.

When it got night outside, she closed her door and made
a fire; then she took off her shoes and put her feet up on the

stool, and that's when Mrs. Lovewright knew that there was something and she didn't have it.

"There's no being cozy without a cat," Mrs. Lovewright said to Dylan from the grocery. "You get around," she said. "I don't care what color so it's little and cute and purrs on my lap."

Next time Dylan came with Mrs. Lovewright's groceries, he brought her a cat. It sat on the floor and held its head at a cute angle.

Mrs. Lovewright tilted her head and said, "Aw! You are so little, I don't believe it!"

Dylan stood in the door, chewed gum, and said, "Whatchu goin callem?"

"Purrly," answered Mrs. Lovewright, "because he's going to lie on my lap and purr, aren't you!" she said to the cat.

Purrly yawned.

Dylan said, "Look at the mouth on that bitty cat."

Mrs. Lovewright looked. She was surprised how wide Purrly's mouth opened, and how many teeth there were inside, like so many little white needles. She said, "So *cute*!"

Purrly lifted his little tail, turned, and would have walked out the door if Dylan hadn't caught and brought him back inside.

"Thank you, Dylan, and good-bye," said Mrs. Lovewright. "Shut the door behind you."

"You and I," she said to Purrly, "are going to be cozy," and she poked the fire, took off her shoes, and said, "Hey! That is my stool you're sitting on! That's for me to put my feet up. You have to lie on my lap."

But Purrly folded his paws under him, settled his little chest, and laid his tail as far as it would go around himself.

"Don't you look cozy!" Mrs. Lovewright said, and smiled into Purrly's eyes. The cat stared at Mrs. Lovewright. He didn't smile back. Mrs. Lovewright was surprised. She sat and she watched Purrly's round, baby-blue eyes close into two blue hyphens. When they had disappeared, Mrs. Lovewright sighed and said, "Chilly in here! I'm going to bed and get under my blanket."

"Be a good looker!" said Dylan in the doorway.

"And so *cute*!" Mrs. Lovewright said.

Purrly lifted his tail and turned and walked away.

"Independent!" said Mrs. Lovewright. "He walks here and he walks there! He thinks this is his house. Shut the door behind you, Dylan, so he can't get out."

"Let's you and me be cozy," Mrs. Lovewright said, and poked the fire and took off her shoes, and she picked Purrly up and put him on her lap and said, "Lie down and I will stroke your back and you purr. You are so warm and so soft! I don't believe how soft you are! Isn't this cozy? Purr! Come on. Don't you know how to purr? You have to go RRR rrr, RRR up, rrr down. Now you. RRR rrr. Try. Lie down. Don't you turn up your tail at me in that rude way!

"Where are you going?"

"Ouch!" Mrs. Lovewright cried, because the cat was running down her leg with his claws out. Then he went and sat and looked at the door and meowed.

"Cat is growing," Dylan said.

"Big enough you'd think he'd know to purr!" said Mrs. Lovewright. "Purrless, that's what I am going to call him! He doesn't know how."

"He knows how to purr," said Dylan. "It's he doesn't want to."

"Good-bye, Dylan. Close the door behind you. And I don't mean *you*!" she told the cat. "You're not going anywhere."

   Mrs. Lovewright
poked the fire and took
her shoes off. "Why don't you
want to purr?" she asked him. "Why?"
And she nudged him with her stocking foot.
"Why? Why? Why? Why?"
   That Purrless flipped onto his back, embraced Mrs.
Lovewright's ankle, held it with his claws, and his tail
flailed to and fro.

He pounded her heel with his back paws and opened his mouth
and bit her little toe. "OUCH!" Mrs. Lovewright hollered
and shook her foot, and that cat flew through
the air, landed on Mrs. Lovewright's broom,
which fell and hit her in the head.

"Cat is twice the size," said Dylan. He stood in the door and chewed and studied her black eye.

"He walks and the floor creaks! You hit me!" Mrs. Lovewright said to Purrless. "You scratched me, and you bit my toe. That isn't nice!" she told him.

"He's a nice cat," Dylan said.

"No, he's not," Mrs. Lovewright said. "A cat that
doesn't purr is not so nice! I don't even *care*,"
she said to Purrless after Dylan shut the door
behind him. "I don't even *want* you lying on
my lap!" She poked the fire, sat down in
her chair, and said, "Get off my stool."
But Purrless folded his paws under him,
settled his chest, and laid his tail
around himself.
"All right, so I'll go to bed!" said Mrs.
Lovewright. "Don't!" she said. The cat
was looking at her stocking foot and
his tail flicked to and fro. "Stop it!"
The cat's eyes were round and yellow;
they stared at Mrs. Lovewright's little toe.
"I want to go to bed and get under my
blanket," Mrs. Lovewright said. "It's chilly!
Why won't you let me get into
my bed?"
Purrless's tail flicked to
and fro and to and fro.
"That is mean," said Mrs.
Lovewright. "I can't
believe how mean you
are!" She sat and she
watched Purrless's eyes
close into two yellow
hyphens, but they did
not disappear.

Mrs. Lovewright sat up in her chair. The fire was out and the cat gone. "Purrless?" cried Mrs. Lovewright. "Where's my pussycat!" And then she saw Purrless curled and enormous, right in the middle of her bed.

"Move yourself over," Mrs. Lovewright told him. That cat didn't budge. Mrs. Lovewright went to push him with her hand and felt how warm he was, and soft, and Mrs. Lovewright stroked his back. She lay down on the bed, right at the edge. The blanket didn't even cover.

She woke with a bump on the floor. "Hey!" Mrs. Lovewright said. "You pushed me!" Purrless was standing on the bed and yawned.

"That is one big cat," said Dylan. He looked at Mrs. Lovewright's arm.

"And mean," Mrs. Lovewright said.

"He's not mean," said Dylan.

"He is, too, mean! He pushed me out of bed!" she said. "He sleeps on my stool so I can't put my feet up. He sits at the door and meows, but will he lie on my lap? He will not! And he won't even let me stroke his back!"

"Yes, he will," Dylan said.

"Yes! when he's *asleep*!" said Mrs. Lovewright.

"He will let you," Dylan said, and squatted down and said, "Here, cat," and he stroked Purrless's back and scratched between his ears.

"He lets *me*," said Dylan.

"Good-bye!" Mrs. Lovewright said to Dylan. "I'm not talking to you!" she told Purrless, and she went and poked that fire and sat in her chair. Then she got up. She went and she grabbed hold of Purrless, put him on her lap, and held him down, and not gently either, and she stroked his back.

"Purr!" Mrs. Lovewright shouted. "See!" she said. "You like it! Isn't this cozy?" She didn't see the cat's tail flicking to and fro and to and fro. "Are you purring?" she said, and when she bent her head to listen, Purrless bit her in the nose.

"Ow!" Mrs. Lovewright hollered. "Ouch!" she yelled. The cat was clawing down her leg. He went and sat down by the door and yowled, and Mrs. Lovewright rose, opened the door, and said, "Get out!"

"Where is the cat?" Dylan asked Mrs. Lovewright, chewing and staring at the Band-Aid on her nose.

"I wouldn't know, and I don't even care," Mrs. Lovewright said. "There's no being cozy with a cat. Shut the door, Dylan, and good-bye."

Then Mrs. Lovewright made a fire, took off her shoes, and put her feet up on her stool. When she went to go to bed nobody bit her toe. She lay down and had the blanket to herself, and that's when she heard Purrless "Meow! Meow! Meow!" right outside the door.

Mrs. Lovewright cozied in.

"Meow! Meow! Meow! Meow!"

"No!" said Mrs. Lovewright.

"Yowl! Yowl! Yowl! Yowl!"

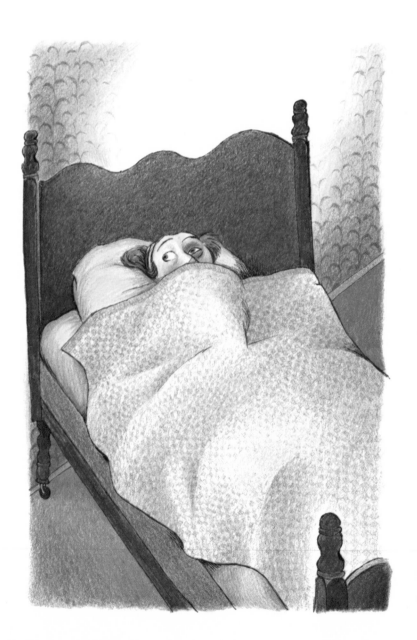

"You don't have to *shout*," said Mrs. Lovewright. She got out of the bed, and went and opened the door. Purrless came streaking in, right between Mrs. Lovewright's legs, jumped on the broom, which fell and tripped Mrs. Lovewright so that Purrless got into the bed ahead of her and curled himself right in the middle of the blanket.

And that's how
Mrs. Lovewright and her cat
lived many years together.

"That is some enormous cat," said Dylan.
"Getting fat!" Mrs. Lovewright said. "Put your feet
together! Look at the rude way you're sitting!"

And she'd go and she would make a fire, sit in her chair, and say, "You're not going to bite my toe, because I'm keeping my shoes on, so there! You could lie on my lap," she'd say, "if you would like."

But that cat would fold his paws, settle his great chest, and curl his tail all the way around himself. His eyes closed, and that's when Mrs. Lovewright would put out her hand and scratch between his ears.

Sometimes she was sure that she heard Purrless purring, and she would look and see the end of his tail flicking to and fro. "Don't you *want* to be cozy?" she would ask him, and she'd stroke his soft, warm, enormous back and she'd say, "*Why* don't you want to?"